This book belongs to:

_____

Special thanks to Joshua and Caia — D.B.

To Franceschino — M.C.

First published in Great Britain in 2022 by Andersen Press Ltd., 20 Vauxhall Bridge Road, London SW1V 2SA Vijverlaan 48, 3062 HL Rotterdam, Nederland Originally published by Tundra Books, a division of Penguin Random House Canada Limited.
Printed and bound in China. 1 3 5 7 9 10 8 6 4 2
ISBN 978 1 83913 228 5

Whose Poo?

DAISY BIRD
MARIANNA COPPO

Now, what are
you not going
to do?

We're
definitely not
going to talk
about poo!

A

ANDERSEN PRESS

Time to get ready now, you two.
I'm going to take you to the zoo.
But only if you're good . . .
which means no talking about poo!

Pssst! What kind of poo
would an astronaut do?

Shiny, silver, space-age poo!
Rocket-powered, weightless poo,
and it spins round and round
like a planet does too!

What kind of poo
would that little dog do?

Tiny, pink, pom-pom poo!
The same kind of poo
that the lady would do!

What kind of poo
would the head chef do?

He does gourmet poo!
On a big china plate — it's teensy-weensy,
but takes ages to do!

And he has to arrange it
in a puddle of goo!

BUS →

Do you think the balloon seller does bendy poo?

He does poo you can
twist into something new!
Squeaky, bendy, blow-up poo!
And it bursts if you step on it
with your shoe!

BUS STOP

BUS STOP

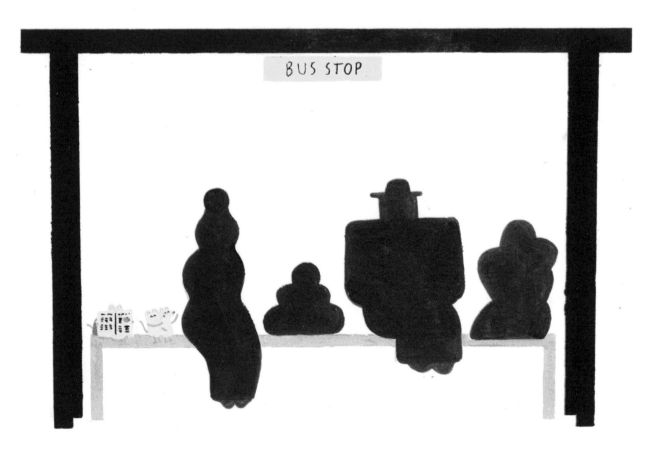

Look at that man with all the tattoos!
What kind of poo would that man do?

Inky, stinky, doesn't-wash-off poo!
With skulls and mermaids and roses too,
and all kinds of things that somebody drew!

What kind of poo
would the ice cream
scooper do?

ZOO

Here we are! Now we can learn all about the animals in the zoo . . .

Think of all
the different
kinds of poo!

There's every poo you could ever do!

I can't match them up. Can you?

What kinds of poo
would these reptiles do?

Chameleons do sneaky camouflage poo!
They can hide it anywhere they
want to!

And pythons do
deadly dangerous poo!
It snakes around behind
and then it squishes you!

What kinds of poo
would the penguins do?

Sparkly, frosty, South Pole poo!
And they build little snow people
out of it too!

What kind of poo would
a blue whale do?

This is what they do
with all the poo.
It makes the trees grow and
the fruits and flowers too.
Take a look around
at what a poo can do!

Wow!
Who knew?